CW00524906

Planet of the Wage Slaves

J. Manfred Weichsel

Published by J. Manfred Weichsel, 2022.

Table of Contents

Chapter 1

Approaching footsteps echoed off the walls of the outside hall. I crouched defensively in the far corner of my cell, watching the door intently as I waited in dread. I shuddered with terror as I heard the creak of a key turning in the lock. The iron door swung open with a loud groan, revealing the serious, solemn faces of the warden and three guards standing behind him.

The warden said, "Come on, Richard. It's time."

I did not leave my defensive crouch. The guards stepped into the cell. I pressed my feet to the floor and pushed my back against the far wall. Cautiously, the guards made their approach.

"Have a heart!" I pleaded. "You can't do this."

The warden gave me the stern look wardens give condemned men everywhere. "Come on, Richard," he said. "You knew this was coming."

With tears streaming down my cheeks I begged, "No! You're too early. I still got time!"

The front most guard reached his hand out as if asking me to take it, gave me a pitying look, and said, "Come on, don't make this any harder on yourself."

"I won't go without a fight," I shouted, and thrashed my arms around blindly to keep the guards back.

The warden said, "Get him."

The three guards grabbed me. I screamed, "No! No! No! You can't! I'm a human being!"

The guards dragged me, kicking and screaming, to the door of my cell. I grabbed onto the side of the metal doorway. "I'm not ready," I cried. "I got rights!"

Two guards pulled at my feet, trying to pry my hands from the metal doorframe, but my grip was too strong for them to break. I was now suspended horizontally in the air, my body stretched like a torture victim on the rack.

The warden said, "Let go of the door, Richard. You've had plenty of time to prepare."

The two guards counted "One, two, three," and gave my legs a big tug. I lost my grip on the doorframe, and all three of us tumbled back into a pile. I jumped to my feet, ran back into my cell, and slammed the door behind me.

I heard the creak of the lock again and the warden opened the cell door. He dove into my cell, tackled me, and held me to the ground. The guards leapt to their feet and ran into the cell. They lifted me into the air.

With two guards taking my arms and the warden and third guard taking my legs, they carried me from the cell feet first, and continued down the dark and foreboding hall as I tried to squirm my way from their grip.

Sweat poured from my brow as we neared the end of the corridor. The eyes on my upturned face were glued to the approaching door. "No! No! No! I don't want to go." I cried. "It's not my time."

The warden and guard released my feet. The other two guards held me upright as I stood there on limp legs. The warden put a key into the lock and turned it, slowly. I cried out, "Please, I don't want to die!"

The warden opened the door and the three guards pushed me into the prison lobby. Worn and tired people sat on benches, waiting impatiently for who-knows-what. A guard asked, "Who said anything about you dying?"

I looked at him with tears streaming down my cheeks. "What will I eat?" I cried. "Where will I sleep? I'm going to die out there."

"You'll just have to get a job and be a productive member of society," the guard replied.

"I don't want a job, "I shouted. "I don't want to be productive!"

The warden and three guards half-dragged me to a counter, behind which sat a clerk. He reached into a cubbyhole, took out a small bag with my personal items, and returned them to me one by one. I didn't even bother to look at the objects as he handed them to me. I couldn't believe this was really happening.

The warden and guards dragged me to a pair of double doors that led outside.

I looked at my feet and mumbled, "I can't survive out there, with all those maniacs. They'll kill me. The maniacs will kill me!"

The warden opened the double doors and one guard snidely said, "Congratulations, Richard. You're a free man."

I thrashed around and screamed, "No! No! No! I don't want to leave," as the guards tossed me through the double doors into the cursed outside.

I jumped to my feet and quickly rushed the doors to get back inside, but the warden was faster. By the time I grabbed the handle he had already locked them.

I heard through the bullet-proof glass as one of the guards said, more to himself than to anybody in particular, "Well, he's the outside world's problem now, not ours."

The warden replied to the guard, "Thank God. That guy was trouble."

I shouted through the glass, "You can't keep me away forever! I'll be back, you hear me? I will be back!"

Chapter 2

I made my way from the prison, which was in downtown Los Angeles, on foot, and by noon I had reached the Walk of Fame, in Hollywood, where tourists, derelicts, homeless teenagers, and maniacs went about doing their thing. I leaned against the gate of the Pantages Theater and watched the crowd pass by, not at all happy to be one of them. I called out to a man who was passing by, "Hey man, can you spare any change?"

The man glanced at me furtively, looked away, muttered, "Sorry," and quickened his pace.

Thinking that perhaps if I got into a fight I would be arrested and sent back to prison, I shouted back in a voice mocking the man's, "Sorry."

The man stopped in his tracks, turned to me indignantly, and said, "Excuse me?"

I shouted, "Fuck you!"

The man, furious, stepped right up to me and with his face inches from mine shouted, "No. Fuck you!"

I shoved the man. "No, fuck you!"

The man punched me in the face. "No! Fuck you!"

We got into a punching match, and the man was winning when two cops rushed over, pulled him off me, and cuffed him.

I was in disbelief. "Hey," I shouted, "I started this fight! I'm the derelict. I was breaking the law by panhandling! You should be arresting me!"

One of the cops turned to me and asked, "Would you like to press charges against this criminal who attacked you?"

I threw my hands into the air, cried out in disgust, and stormed off through bumper-to-bumper traffic towards the W hotel on the other side of Hollywood Blvd. I looked back occasionally to see if the cop was going to follow and arrest me for jaywalking, but he was preoccupied arresting the other man. It wasn't fair!

Outside the metro at the entrance to the W, a drug dealer walked by a crowd of derelicts whispering, "Weed, meth, crack, smack, pills."

I watched with interest as a young man stopped the drug dealer and said, "Hey, man."

The drug dealer turned to the young man and said, "Weed, meth, crack, smack, pills."

The young man pulled out a badge.

The drug dealer muttered, "Shit, man," as he was cuffed and brought around the corner towards two parked squad cars.

I contemplated what I had just witnessed for a moment. Drug dealing! So, that was the ticket to prison. I walked into the middle of a crowd of passersby and called, "Weed, meth, crack, smack, pills."

A young man walked up to me and said, "Hey, man."

I turned to the young man and said, "Weed, meth, crack, smack, pills."

The young man pulled a crumpled bill from his pocket, shoved it into my hand, and said, "What can I get for twenty dollars?"

I looked at the young man in disbelief, shoved him, shouted, "Fuck you, man," and ran off with the twenty-dollar bill. But nobody chased me.

I headed east away from the Walk of Fame until I reached the liquor store on the corner of Hollywood and Bronson and went inside. I glanced around quickly. The store was empty except for the owner, an Indian guy, who was stocking shelves with snacks. The liquor was behind the counter.

I made a run for the counter, dove over it, grabbed a pint of cheap whiskey, jumped back over the counter, and made a run for the exit.

The owner turned, shouted "Hey," rushed me, and grabbed me before I reached the door.

With a grin on my face I said, "What are you going to do? Call the cops and have me arrested?"

The owner responded, "Fuck you, man," frisked me, took the twenty dollar bill out of my pants pocket, put it in his own, lifted me by the back of my collar and the back of my pants, and swung me back and forth to build up momentum.

I said, "Aren't you going to give me my change?" as the owner hurled me, still grasping the bottle of whisky, out the door onto the hard pavement.

I hadn't had a drink in a long time, so, sitting outside the liquor store where I had landed, I opened the bottle, brought it to my lips, and took a long swig.

I got to my feet, crossed Bronson, and stood outside the Tommy's Hamburgers there as I quickly downed half of the pint-sized bottle.

In the parking lot, sitting on the stoop in front of the entrance to Tommy's, was another bum drinking whisky from a bottle. Customers stepped over and around him as they entered and exited the restaurant. A squad car pulled up in front of this bum and two cops got out, took his bottle, and put him in cuffs.

I tilted my head back and let out a piercing wail. "Wahahahaha!!! Why can't I get arrested??? Maniacs!!! They're all maniacs out here!!!"

I took another long swig and walked down Hollywood Boulevard wailing loudly and drinking. "Whahahahaha!!!!!!!"

I reached the overpass that goes over the Hollywood freeway. I chugged the rest of the bottle, tossed it into the weeds at the side of the road, wiped my mouth with the back of my hand, let out a wail, and stumbled across the ramp to the overpass.

I stepped over the curb and climbed down off the sidewalk, crossed over the weeds, and climbed up onto the overpass, on the side of the fence that faced the freeway.

My palms turned back, I held onto the chain link fence with my fingers. Facing the freeway, with the heels of my feet on the narrow strip of cement, I inched my way to the middle of the overpass. I looked straight ahead at the Hollywood sign in the distance and then down at the cars rushing by and cried out, "Whahaha!!! Wahaha!!!!"

From the corner of my eye I saw a man walk by on the sidewalk behind me. He gave me a furtive glance, picked up his pace, and crossed the overpass quickly without giving me another look. I saw the man hurry off out the corner of my other eye and screamed, "Ahahahaha!!! Maniacs!!!"

Below me, a car swerved through two lanes of traffic, cutting off the other cars on the freeway, and zoomed up the exit ramp.

The car screeched to a halt, parking illegally on the overpass, and a beautiful woman dressed in a sharp business suit ran right up to me. I was about to jump when she shouted, "No! Don't! Your life has meaning! You can be a hero!"

I shouted back in anguish, "I don't want to be a hero! I don't en want to be alive!!!"

"Why? What could make life so unbearable?"

Sobbing, I said, "Do you have a special place, a place where ou can be safe and alone?"

She said, "Of course I do. Everybody does."

"I can never go back to mine!"

"Why can't you go back?"

Tears streamed down my face. I screamed at the top of my ngs as all the suffering I had endured was released, "Because ve been rehabilitated!!!"

More cars parked illegally on the overpass and the sidewalk came crowded with people. A chubby African American man a dress shirt, slacks, and tie paced back and forth on the lewalk behind the beautiful woman muttering, "Oh Dear od, don't let him jump. Not today. Oh dear God, not today."

The woman said, "Please! Climb back over the fence. I need talk to you. I need you to save my people."

I cried, "I hate talking and I hate people. Ohhhh!!! Ahhh!!! vant to die!"

The beautiful woman shouted in a voice that was choked up th tears, "But I can show you that your life has purpose!"

I removed one hand from the fence, leaned forward, and inted at the cars below my feet zooming south. "Look at all ose cars passing by. Each one is driven by a person. Each one those people can see me standing here on this ledge! And they n't care that I am about to jump. None of them care!"

The African American quickened his pace and muttered, Vhy don't they stop the traffic? Oh dear God, why don't they p the traffic???"

The woman pleaded, "But I stopped. I care!"

I cried back, "But you're a just a stupid yuppie. Oh Go[d] nobody cares."

The woman waved her arms towards the crowd of onlooke[rs] on the shoulder of the overpass. "Look at all these people w[ho] have stopped! They all care!"

With my free hand, I pointed at a group of Mexica[n] teenagers who were drinking malt liquor as they chanted, "Jum[p!] Jump! Jump! Jump!"

I screamed, "Do they look like they care?"

I pointed to a bald white guy standing outside a news va[n] holding a large television camera on his shoulder, which w[as] pointed at the freeway at my feet. "And him! He just wants a sh[ot] of my body as it hits the pavement!"

The woman pointed at the African American man. S[he] shouted, "Look at him! He cares!"

I craned my neck to look at the African American paci[ng] back and forth as he muttered, "Oh, God. Oh, dear God. I ha[ve] the most important job interview of my life today. Please Go[d] don't let him jump. Not now. Not today."

I screamed, "You see??? The only reason he doesn't wa[nt] me to jump is that it will upset him before his job intervi[ew] and he won't get hired. Ahahahah! He's a maniac!!! They're [all] maniacs!!!! Ohhhh!!! Ahhhh!!!!!"

The woman said, "Listen, you have to help me. My name [is] Destiny, and I am not from here. I have gone up and down, ba[ck] and forth from one end of this small planet you call Los Ange[les] to the other, looking for someone like you. I have explor[ed] Venice Beach, Santa Monica, Downtown LA, Silver Lake, a[nd]

Echo Park, and came up with zilch. My people are being oppressed, and only you can save them!"

"I don't want to save your people! Ahhhh!!! Ohhhh!!!"

I stopped screaming and looked down at the hard pavement below. While Destiny had been pleading with me not to jump, fire trucks and police cars had arrived and were closing the Hollywood freeway. I knew it was now or never.

I slowly relaxed the grip of my fingers on the metal fence and leaned forward towards the freeway.

Destiny cried, "No!"

She stuck out a wand with a marble-sized orb on its end, and a glowing portal appeared beneath me, halfway between the overpass and the pavement. It shimmered and sparkled with orange, yellow, and white light. Frightened, I scrambled to regain my footing on the ledge, but it was too late. I fell into the portal.

Chapter 3

I flew headfirst, waving my arms frantically in front of me as trails of orange, yellow, and white light zoomed by. I shut my eyes and screamed, "Ahahahaha!!!!!"

I landed with a thud, and when I opened my eyes, I was seated in a musty old office chair surrounded on three sides by the particleboard of an office cubicle.

I looked around, confused. It was just an ordinary cubicle, a bit disorganized, with a desk, note pads, pens, and papers strewn around an old desktop computer. A woman poked her head into the cubicle and said, "Are you okay in there? We heard a noise."

"Where am I?" I asked.

The woman let out a single laugh and said, "Wouldn't we all like to know!"

"But, how did I get here?"

The woman laughed again and said, "I ask myself the same question each and every morning!"

"Where's Destiny?"

"The answer is different for everybody, but I certainly hope it's not here. Well, I'll talk to you later, Roger."

I wrinkled my brow in confusion and said, "My name's not Roger."

"That's funny. I could have sworn it was. Oh, I get it. You're playing one of your little jokes."

The woman gave a fake chuckle, as if she didn't want to encourage me but thought it would be impolite not to laugh, and then said, "Well, take care."

She ducked out of the cubicle and was gone.

I sat there trying to make sense of everything when a man of about fifty with perfect hair, perfect teeth, a big, open, round face, and the build of an amateur weightlifter, stepped into the cubicle and speaking in a rude and abrupt manner said, "Roger, I need you to enter this data into a spreadsheet."

He held out a stack of papers. I didn't take them and just looked at him blankly.

He said, "Roger?"

I shouted, "Richard!"

He said, "Who is Richard? Roger, I need you to enter this into a spreadsheet."

He shoved the papers into my hands. I looked at them and then looked back up at the man. "But this is a spreadsheet," I said.

"Let me repeat myself," he said impatiently. "I need you to enter this spreadsheet into a spreadsheet. You have until eleven o'clock. Good day."

The boss man turned abruptly and left. I looked at the papers and muttered to myself, "This is fucking bullshit. Enter a spreadsheet into a spreadsheet. This sucks. No fucking way am I doing this shit. It already is a spreadsheet. Bullshit!"

I threw the papers down onto the desk to the side of the keyboard and left the cubicle. I looked around at the tired, haggard, ash-colored faces of overworked, underpaid, and underfed wage slaves. Some were in cubicles like mine. Others sat in a row of chairs along a single long desk against the wall.

I ducked out of the office and walked down the hall quickly, until I came to two elevator banks.

Standing there was another man, waiting. When I stopped next to him to wait for an elevator, he turned, and seeming to recognize me, said, "Morning, Roger."

I said, "Richard."

The man said, "No. I'm Gary. God, this place sucks. I don't blame you for not knowing my name. We all blend together here, don't we? You seen the bathroom today? Asshole put paper towels in the waterless urinal again. Motherfucker! Doesn't whoever it is know he's not hurting the establishment? He's hurting us, his fellow workers. So, how's your day been?"

I was impatient for the elevator to arrive, and wished to avoid small talk. But, knowing etiquette dictated that I had to answer with something, I shrugged and said, "Oh, just another day at the rat race, I guess."

Gary laughed. "Rat race! Ha! I love it! This place isn't a race. It's a God damned hamster wheel. And here we are, we run and we run, and the wheel spins under our feet, but we don't go anywhere, and we keep on running and running until we tucker out and die. Why do we do it, Roger? Why don't we just jump off the damned wheel?"

The elevator opened and an impossibly old man tumbled out onto the ratty carpet. He said in a reedy voice, "Is this the one millionth floor?"

I looked at the sign on the wall and said, "No, it's floor one thousand and thirteen."

The old man broke into tears of despair. "When I stepped into this elevator on floor one thousand and ten, I was a young man of twenty five. All I wanted was to see the mythical penthouse suite, spoken about only in legend, where the CEOs of yore are said to still live. I wanted to know if they really existed, and if the stories were true."

The man was lying on the ground, trying to stand, but he was so old that getting up required too much exertion. Now, gave up trying and just lay there. His gaze softened, as if he was peering beyond the confines of the hall, and he continued, "Three floors. I only made it three floors. And it took me a lifetime to get here."

The old man died.

Gary exclaimed, "They really need to install faster elevators in this place," as he stepped into the elevator. When I didn't follow he added, impatiently, "Aren't you coming?"

Looking for an excuse I said, "Uh, no... I'm going down."

He said, "Well, I've got to deliver this report to floor one thousand and fourteen." Then he added in a mock-cheerful voice, "See you in another life."

The elevator doors shut and I stood in the hall, alone. "Fuck the elevators," I said.

I walked quickly down the hall looking for a way out of the horrible place. In a normal building, the hall would have ended in another one going at a right angle. But where this hall ended many halls began, going out in all different directions like spokes in a wheel. I picked one that went back at about a twenty-degree angle from the way I had come.

This new hall looped around at the end, and I found myself back at the elevators. I ran down another hall and continued through a twisting labyrinth. I stopped, leaned against a wall, panted to catch my breath, and saw to my horror that I was once again back at the elevators.

An office door opened, and Destiny came running out into the hall. She cried, "Richard!"

I said, "You know my name."

She said, "Of course I do. I am sure you have a lot of questions."

"I do. And my first is, where am I, and why does everybod
here call me Roger?"

She said, "Certain people on your planet, Los Angeles, sha
bio signatures with people within this office planet. I was on L
searching for somebody whose bio signature corresponded wi
that of somebody's here without luck until I drove beneath yo
standing on the overpass above the Hollywood freeway, and th
bio reader in my car told me that yours corresponded to that
this planet's Roger. So I sent you through the portal and in
Roger's body, so you can save my people. Have you looked in
mirror since you arrived here?"

"Uh, I don't think so."

"Well, don't be too shocked next time you use the restroor
You are in somebody else's body."

"Why go through all this trouble? Why not just ask Rog
to save your people?"

"Because, although he thinks himself a rebel, Roger
actually a loyal employee, and would side with Goodwyn."

"Well, I've only been here a short while and I've already m
a few disgruntled employees. Why not ask one of them?"

"Because their spirits are broken, so they wouldn't be able
stand up to Goodwyn."

"But my spirit is broken too. I've spent most of my adult li
in prison and I'm suicidal."

"That still gives you more spirit than the people who wo
here."

I said, "Reluctantly, from what I have seen, I have to adn
that this is true. Okay, I will save your people. Tell me about th
Goodwyn you keep mentioning."

Destiny said, "Goodwyn is a boss. A very, very bad boss..."

But she was interrupted when a voice came on through an intercom and announced, "Will all employees please meet promptly in the auditorium for a company-wide meeting."

Destiny said, "Shit, we have to go. Absence from a company-wide meeting means a day in the stockades! Come on. We must hurry."

She took my hand and led me off. I couldn't help but notice how nice and warm her hand felt.

Chapter 4

We entered a huge auditorium full of office workers buzzing loudly to one another. It was so crowded that Destiny and I had to look around for two seats together.

The man from before who had told me to enter a spreadsheet into a spreadsheet stepped out onto the stage and everybody hushed.

Destiny whispered, "That is Goodwyn."

Speaking in a forced tone, like a 1920's European fascist giving a speech, Goodwyn said, "Greetings everybody, and welcome. Thank you for being here. I have some good news. Thanks to the work you all have done, campaign GNW998B came in 13% above goal in performance and a whopping 28% above goal in speed last week, so cumulatively, we are only negative 15% on performance and negative 2% on speed.

"Competition is cumulatively at negative 10% on performance; performance is the metric the client cares about because that's where they make their money, and if we can keep this up, we will have passed the competition on performance by this week's end!"

The audience applauded fervently, but it was with a fake sort of passion, as if rather than being true zealots, they were simply afraid to come across as unenthusiastic.

Goodwyn's tone darkened as he continued, "But the competition is far ahead of us on speed. They are cumulatively at plus 30%, whereas with all the work we did last week, we haven't even gotten out of the negative. Speed is where this company gets paid, and corporate profit as a whole continues to slide deeper and deeper into the fiery pits of the red."

Goodwyn pointed a wooden pointer at a chart depicting a zigzagging red line traveling downwards into flames. He continued, "Without corporate profit, this company can't pay you. If this company can't pay you, we will have to let you go. And without jobs, you will all die. That is why speed is so important.

"But I am still seeing things like people taking unscheduled breaks to use the restroom, get water, and talk to your coworkers. All of this hurts speed. Unscheduled breaks must stop!"

A big burly shirtless man in trousers held up by black, spiked leather suspenders, his head covered by a black hood, dragged with one giant hand a trembling little old man from the wing to center stage, and forced him to the ground.

In his other hand, the big burly man held an axe.

Goodwyn motioned to the trembling old man and continued, "Many of you know Neil personally. Today I asked Neil to enter data into a spreadsheet by a certain time. Neil was an hour late, hurting speed, and jeopardizing all of your jobs. This is the third time in a row Neil has been late with an assignment, and as you all know, three strikes and you're out."

Goodwyn turned to Neil and said, "Do you have any last words?"

Neil bowed his head and said, "Thank you for the opportunity, sir. I am sorry it didn't work out."

The executioner raised his axe and brought it down, lobbing Neil's head off, which rolled across the stage as a geyser of blood spurted from his neck.

Goodwyn said a few more words imploring us to work more productively so as not to suffer the same fate as Neil. He insisted that he did not like executing workers, because that meant he had to train new ones, which cost the company money, and then closed by telling us to return to our desks, and that as company-wide meetings hurt speed, we were all to work extra-fast the rest of the day to make up for it.

As Destiny and I exited the auditorium, I was too stunned to talk. But the throng of coworkers exiting with us chatted loudly, as if this were a regular occurrence.

Suddenly, I had a horrible thought. I muttered, "My... my... the spreadsheet."

"What's that?" Destiny asked.

"Goodwyn. Earlier he gave me a spreadsheet to enter into a spreadsheet."

Destiny grabbed my arm in a panic. With dread in her voice she asked, "When's it due?"

"Eleven o'clock."

Destiny looked at her watch. "My God. Roger was late with his last two assignments, and it's already 9:45!"

She dragged me down the hall by my arm. After a few minutes we reached the office where I first arrived through the portal, and she shoved me into Roger's cubicle.

She said, "If you don't hand in your assignment on time, it'll be the axe over your neck just like it was Neil's, and Goodwyn will make your head roll. Shit. It's almost 9:50 now."

She turned over an hourglass on the desk and said, "The sand in this glass will last one hour. That will only give you ten minutes to get your assignment to Goodwyn. I am going to go so I don't distract you while you work."

"Wait! I don't really have much office experience. Can't you ͻ the assignment for me?"

"No. The spreadsheet has to have your bio signature. That's hy you were chosen. Your bio signature matches Roger's. ᵗherwise you wouldn't be able to receive credit for his signment and you'd be executed. Good luck. You're going to ᵉed it."

Destiny left and I sat there staring at the black computer ᵣeen. I pressed some keys on the keyboard. Nothing happened. ᴵooked the computer over and muttered, "How do you turn .is damn thing on?"

I fiddled with the mouse. Nothing happened. I got onto my ᴵnds and knees and checked the plugs. They were all plugged . I sat up again and looked at the dead computer, thinking.

I looked up at the sand pouring through the hourglass. Sweat ᵣmed on my brow.

I breathed heavily a couple of times and muttered, "Okay. ᴷay. Okay. I can do this."

I looked back at the computer, determined to solve its riddle. ᴵn the front of the console was an orange switch! Could this be ᵉ secret I was looking for? I flipped the switch. The computer ᴵmmed to life! But now what to do?

The keys on the keyboard pulsated as if inviting me to touch ᵉm. When I reach my hand to the keyboard, my fingers ᵉtched like putty towards the keys. Something was happening, ᴵt whatever it was, I was no longer in control.

When my elongated fingers reached the pulsating keys, my ᴵgertips merged with the fleshy plastic knobs so that they ᶜame one. The keys throbbed as if in excitement as my fingers ᵉlted into them. The rest of my hands slowly sank into the keyboard up to my wrists. One of my eyes stretched toward the monitor. The screen stretched out towards my elongated ey My other eye stretched out of its socket, reaching towards th spreadsheet on the desk to the side of the keyboard where I ha left it.

My one eye melted into the screen. When my other e melted into the spreadsheet, a burst of energy came up fro the stack of papers, traveling up my stretched-out eye, down m body into one arm, through the keyboard, back up my other arr into my skull, and then out through my other eye and into th monitor.

The sensation of all the data flowing through me was s intense that I passed out, but when I returned to consciousne the printer was spitting out page after page of spreadsheet. looked at the hourglass. The last grains of sand were falling to th bottom compartment.

I quickly gathered the pages of spreadsheet from the print tray, made sure that they were in order, and ran from the offi into the halls.

But where was Goodwyn's office? I had no idea. I ran dov a hall, clutching my papers, but the hall ended abruptly.

"Damn it!" I cried.

I turned and ran down another hall. This hall ended abrup too. I muttered, "Why do all of these halls stop at dead end Oh, I get it. It's a dead-end job."

I ran back and turned down another hall. This hall ended a door. I opened the door and at the other end of a large roo sat Goodwyn behind a large mahogany desk.

Out of breath, I said, "I... I... I got you your spreadsheet."

Goodwyn took my papers. "Thank you, Roger, right on time." He smiled as he put the papers down on a tray on his desk. "I'll look this over when I get the chance. In the meantime, I have a meeting today across town at another office planet, so I need a detailed statistical analysis on the probability that it is raining right now so I know whether or not to bring an umbrella."

"Why don't you just look out a window?"

"Because I don't have the time to look out a window! This meeting is with a very important consulting firm and I don't want to show up wet."

It occurred to me that I had not looked out a window since arriving at this strange place. I looked around Goodwyn's office, and there was not a window to be seen! There weren't any windows anywhere in the office building!

Then, I noticed something against a far wall that looked like a porthole on a ship. I pointed to it and said, "Can I look through that... window... and maybe tell you if it's raining or not?"

Goodwyn waved a hand and said, "As you are merely a worker and not executive level like myself, you would not be remotely able to comprehend what you see, but I'm feeling in a good mood so go ahead."

I went to the porthole and, sticking my head into the aperture, peered into the monitor at the other end. What I saw left me in a state of awe. There was no sky above me, and no ground below. Stretching out in all directions was empty space, and hanging suspended in this space were giant orbs. The surfaces of these orbs were like the exteriors of office buildings, and I knew what Destiny had meant when she said that we were within an office planet. Each of the orbs was an office planet just like the one I was in, and inside each one of them, I knew, were armies of wage slaves toiling away for their corporations just as the wage slaves within this office planet were toiling away for ours.

I went back to Goodwyn in a daze.

"Is it raining right now?" He asked.

"I really don't know," I replied.

"See? I knew you weren't able to receive the mysteries of the cosmos. You had better go create that statistical analysis of whether or not it is raining, because the clock is ticking. You have until two o'clock. Good day!"

Chapter 5

Back at my cubicle, I sat staring at the computer, stuck. I didn't know what a statistical analysis was, let alone how to create one. I opened a desk drawer and right there was a textbook titled, "How to create a statistical analysis."

I picked up the book. It was as thick as a phonebook. With dread I opened it and looked at the table of contents. The book was 54 chapters long, and chapter 54 began on page 1,308. This was a long-ass book!

With sweat pouring down my brow, I turned the page to the first chapter and read:

Chapter 1:

An Overview of Statistical Analysis

Welcome to the wild and wonderful world of statistical analysis. Human beings have been using statistical analysis for thousands of years to help accomplish all sorts of important tasks. The first statistical analyses were created over three thousand years ago in ancient China during the Ming Dynasty. The Chinese used statistical analysis in many areas of daily life, from farming, to trade, to palace administration.

Well, humanity has progressed a lot since then, and today modern humans use statistical analysis in exciting new ways that could have never been dreamt about by the ancient Chinese. No doubt you have already encountered statistical analysis in many areas of your own personal life. Perhaps, for example, you have come across statistical analyses in the sports section of your local newspaper.

In this book, you will learn everything you need to know to be empowered to create statistical analyses of your own. Statistical analysis is a great tool to have in your employee toolbox, and a study by The Institute for Statistical Analysis recently showed that by learning statistical analysis, you can potentially increase your earning power by up to 15% over the lifetime of your career. By deciding to read this book, you have made the "statistically" right choice!

My eyes glazed over with boredom as I read and I was just starting to nod off when Destiny ran into my cubicle jolting me awake and cried, "Richard, we need you now! Goodwyn is on a tear! He's out of control. There's no telling what he's going to do."

I said, "But I have work to do. Oh my God, what time is it? Goodwyn said I needed to complete this by two o'clock."

Destiny said, "It doesn't matter. Just skip it."

"Skip it!!!" I cried. "But I'll be beheaded!"

"No, you won't. You're only executed if you are late with three assignments in a row. You got the last one in on time, right, else you wouldn't be here, so it reset itself and there's no point doing this one."

"Wait a minute. You're telling me that you only have to do every third assignment?"

"Yeah, but that's a bad habit to get into because you might skip two and then be late with the third through circumstances beyond your control, and then your head's rolling across the floor!"

"But seriously, how do they keep people from blowing off the other two assignments?"

"They don't. They just assign busy work for the two freebees and save the stuff they really need done for when it counts."

"Okay. Let's go. But first I have to tell you, I love you."

Destiny gave me a serious look and said, "I love you too."

We kissed. It was a quick kiss, as there wasn't a lot of time, but it was electrifying.

Just as we broke off, Goodwyn stormed into the office screaming, "I am furious at all of you!"

The tired, ashen, hungry faces of the other wage slaves turned forward and looked at Goodwyn blankly.

He shouted, "This is the third day in a row that my lunch has been stolen out of the refrigerator. If you are hungry, there is a sheet of paper on the refrigerator door that lists food pantry planets, shelter planets, and church planets that give out free food. Do you all know how lucky you are to work for a company that provides you with information on where to get free food?"

One worker said, "But that list disappeared over a year ago."

Goodwyn shouted, "Then you should have told your supervisor and he would have replaced it."

Another worker said, "But what good does a list of plane[s] do us when we can't leave this one?"

Goodwyn pointed at the worker and crie[d] "Insubordination! When we tell you where you can get fr[ee] food, we expect gratitude from you, whether you can use t[he] information or not. We expect you to wake up every mornin[g] grateful to us for the privilege of working here. I know that t[he] culprit knows that it's my lunch that he's been stealing. I label [it] with my name. Well, I want to know who it is."

Goodwyn clapped his hands and cried, "Supervisors!"

Five supervisors with machineguns rushed in and grabbed [a] woman from her desk. They dragged the struggling female to t[he] front of the room. There, they secured chains to both her wris[ts] and put the other ends of the chains through metal loops bolt[ed] to the walls on either side. They pulled on the ends of the chai[ns] that went through the loops so that her arms were stretched [as] far as they would go, and then secured the chains to bolts on t[he] floor. The woman cried and pleaded that she was innocent.

Goodwyn, ignoring her cries, grabbed her blouse and ripp[ed] it off, stripping her to the waist. She was a tall brunette wi[th] auburn eyes, which filled with tears as her full, perky breasts we[re] exposed. Facing the rest of the office, she held her head down [in] shame.

Goodwyn took a whip from his side and let it uncoil. It w[as] a very long whip.

He shouted, "Who is stealing my lunch?"

He was met with silence.

Goodwyn let the whip fly against woman's back. It made [a] loud cracking noise when it hit her, and her entire body arch[ed] and then trembled in shock.

Goodwyn shouted, "I will keep on asking, and every time I don't get an answer, this woman gets a lash."

He brought his arm with the whip back. The woman shut her eyes tight in anticipation of another blow.

Goodwyn shouted, "Now, who is stealing my lunch?"

The wage slaves eyed each other nervously, but none came forward. Goodwyn let the whip fly. Crack! A mist of blood sprayed from the woman's back when the whip hit it, and little droplets hung in the air. The woman's body shook convulsively, and on her face was a look of excruciating pain.

This continued for many more blows, with Goodwyn demanding someone tell him who was stealing his lunch, and punishing the poor woman each time he was met with silence. Each time Goodwyn whipped her, the spray of blood became thicker, and her convulsions heavier, until at last Goodwyn whipped her and she didn't move at all.

A supervisor checked her pulse. "She's dead," he said.

"I know," said Goodwyn. "Grab another one so we can continue."

The supervisors grabbed Destiny and dragged her to the front to the room. They unchained the dead woman, letting her body fall to the ground, and put the chains around Destiny's wrists. Goodwyn stripped Destiny to the waist. She held her head bravely high.

Goodwyn, standing behind Destiny with his whip, shouted, "Who is stealing my lunch?"

Destiny closed her eyes and waited for in inevitable. But I was in love with Destiny. I could not allow her to be whipped. I could not let her die.

With a cry of rage, I rushed Goodwyn to tackle him. But before I reached him, the supervisors all turned their guns on me, and I felt many bullets rip through my body.

When I woke up, I was lying in a hospital bed. A male nurse was there. He said, "Ah. You're awake."

I noticed right away that my body was not riddled with bullet holes, so I asked, "How did I get here?"

He said, "By the time you jumped, the emergency responders had set up a trampoline beneath you, so instead of hitting the pavement, you bounced a couple of times. You passed out from fright, I guess, but other than a few bumps and bruises you're perfectly fine."

"I guess I'm pretty lucky," I said.

"Oh, I wouldn't say that," he said.

"What do you mean?"

"Your life is over. They stopped the Hollywood freeway because of you. You'll be paying that fine off as long as you live. You're going to wish you had become street pizza."

I looked up at the ceiling and cried. But I was not crying about the inevitable fine. After all, they couldn't take money I didn't have. I was thinking about my Destiny, up there on the office planet, and wondering whether or not she was alive. Perhaps my actions had provided the other wage slaves with enough of a distraction to defeat Goodwyn and liberate the planet from its bad boss. But there was no way I could ever know.

"Destiny!" I cried. "Destiny!"

Chapter 6

The jury threw the book at me. I was found guilty of disorderly conduct, public intoxication, attempted suicide, you name it.

Now, I stood in the courtroom with my head bowed as the judge fined me fifteen million dollars and then concluded, "...And as you do not have the money to pay what you owe to the planet of Los Angeles, I hereby sentence you to community service picking up trash on the side of the Hollywood freeway at minimum wage, which shall be deposited directly into the city coffers, until you have paid off your debt to society."

I said, "But... but minimum wage is fifteen dollars an hour. That means it will take me one million hours."

I turned to my court-appointed attorney and asked, "How many years is that?"

The attorney took out his smart phone, typed something into Google, and said, "One million hours means you will be performing community service for 114.115 years. Of course, that assumes a twenty-four-hour workday, seven days a week."

I looked at the judge and cried, "You can't do this!"

The judge raised an eyebrow and said, "Oh, and why not?"

"It's slavery!"

"And what is wrong with slavery?"

"It's against the constitution!"

"No, it isn't."

"Yes, it is."

"No, it isn't. The constitution literally allows slavery."

"No, it doesn't. We fought a civil war over this."

The judge took a little blue pamphlet from his breast pocket and said, "The constitution happens to be my favorite book. I carry it with me wherever I go, and I know it front and back."

He opened the book and read, "Amendment thirteen, section 1. Neither slavery nor involuntary servitude, except as a punishment for crime whereof the party shall have been duly convicted, shall exist within the United States, or any place subject to their jurisdiction."

He looked up from the book and said, "You see? You have been duly convicted of a crime, several, in fact, so the constitution literally allows me to enslave you."

So, I had no choice but to go work.

Every morning I woke up on my cot in the halfway house, put on my orange jumpsuit, and was bussed with the other slaves to the side of the freeway where, armed with pokers and trash bags, we picked up litter left the night before by passing motorists.

All the while, I continued to think about Destiny, and wonder what had happened to her, and if she was still alive. I wondered if she had defeated the bad boss Goodwyn, and if her people were free.

One day, as I made my way through some bushes to get to some hard-to-reach litter, I saw, hidden behind a bush, a portal! Excited that it might bring me back to the office planet and Destiny, and reasoning that as bad as wage slavery was, the nonwage kind was worse, I jumped into the portal.

Chapter 7

I flew head-first with my arms flailing at my sides, as the white, yellow, and orange sparkling light of the portal rushed past me.

I fell out of the portal at the other end and landed with a thud.

I looked around. I was seated in a chair in a dark room, surrounded on all sides by the silhouettes of people seated as I was, facing forward. This time, nobody noticed the thud as I landed.

An image was projected onto a screen on the front wall. It was some sort of late 19th century romanticist painting depicting a nude woman on a swing. She faced forward, towards the viewer, and was in the middle of pumping her arms back and pushing her legs forward to make the swing go. The background was pastoral, with willow trees growing along the grassy bank of a blue brook. The swing was tied to a tree branch.

The frustrated voice of a fat, single, middle-aged woman angrily lectured the room as she said, "As you can see, this is but another example of the male gaze in art. Notice how the woman is placed on another pedestal, this time a swing. Look at the painting's perspective. The male viewer of the painting is forced to stare right at the woman, who displays her body for his pleasure. It isn't much different from this next work of 'art.'"

She held out a hand and the silhouette of her fat thumb pressed down on a small device connected to a wire. I heard the clicking of slides changing in a slide machine, and the renaissance painting was replaced by a hardcore pornographic photograph of a woman sitting on the ground with her legs spread wide an the pink of her vagina facing the camera.

The fat woman continued, "As you see once again, tho old paintings weren't any more 'artistic' than your typic photograph from Hustler magazine in the 1970's. Notice th the composition of the painting and the photograph are almo identical. Both objectify their female subject and depict tl female body as the landscape on which sexual activity tak place, in order to perpetuate a paradigm of male dominance."

Leaving the pornographic image up on the wall, the wom: walked to the door and flipped the light switch. I blinked n eyes. Once they had adjusted to the harshness of the fluorescen I saw that the fat woman looked as frustrated and angry as s sounded. I wondered what kind of a strange planet I had land on this time.

The others, who were all young, in their late teens or ea twenties, rose from their desks and rushed the door at once, ar a brief traffic jam formed as they bottlenecked exiting the roo as the middle-aged woman said, "Remember, for next week want everybody to bring in six classic paintings and six simila composed pornographic photographs from Hustler magazir accompanied by texts you have written describing all tl similarities you can find between the paintings and photograpl I want you to find at least six similarities for each pair, thirty-six in total, although bonus points for anybody who c find more."

I muttered to myself, "Something tells me I'm not in office planet."

I exited the room, and in the hall right outside, someo who was exiting at the same time said to me, "This class is gre isn't it Ryan? All she does is show us pictures of naked women and tell us we're wrong to look at them. Only thing is, I'm afraid it's going to do me some serious psychological damage."

"Why?" I asked, hoping to get some information that would help me solve the mystery of where I was.

"Well, it's all about guilt. They use it to get you to act how they want. It's totally, like, harmful though."

Just then a beautiful but snobby-looking girl walked by and said, "If by looking at pictures of naked women you are helping to continue two thousand years of female oppression, then you should feel guilty for looking at them."

The snobby girl walked off. The strange young man said, "See what I mean? Well, see you around, Ryan," and then departed.

As I walked alone down the long, wide, crowded hall, I noticed that I was carrying a heavy textbook in one arm. I looked at the cover and read the title, "Making and reading pornographic images."

Curious, I opened the book and read:

Chapter 1:

An Overview of Pornography

Welcome to the wild and wonderful world of pornography. Human beings have been using pornography for thousands of years to help accomplish all sorts of important tasks. The first pornography was created over three thousand years ago in ancient China during the Ming Dynasty. The Chinese used pornography in many areas of daily life, from...

I closed the book, tossed it into the nearest trashcan, and continued to the spacious entrance. I went outside through one of about a dozen doors lined up side-by-side, and looked out onto a wide field, where hundreds of young men and women were lying in the grass, playing hacky sack and Frisbee, reading books, and talking loudly.

The truth of where I was dawned on me. I muttered, "I must have landed on some sort of liberal arts college planet."

I looked around a moment longer and added, "I honestly don't see how this kind of environment is supposed to prepare kids for the real world."

Then, after examining some of the females lying in the grass in their short athletic shorts and at how their nipples poked through their t-shirts with no bras I said, "On the other hand, I kind of like it here."

One of the women made eye contact with me and waved her arms in the air excitedly. She ran up to me energetically shouting, "Ryan! Hey! Ryan!"

The woman reached me. She was earthy, in a loose-fitting hemp shirt and tie-dyed sweatpants.

Having surmised a bit by now about how the universe worked I said, "I'm not Ryan. My name is Richard and I am from another planet called Los Angeles. The reason I am in Ryan's body is because..."

The woman said, "Wow, I must be really, really, really stoned because I thought you just said... What did you say? Oh yeah, Ryan, hey, we need your help. It's an emergency. Come on."

She tugged at my hand and pointed to a bench where a longhaired, sensitive-looking man sat.

The woman said, "Look!"

Not knowing what I was supposed to be looking at I said, "What?"

"It's Jerry! Sitting on that bench, all alone."

I shrugged my shoulders. "So?"

"So, doesn't he look a little sad?"

"I guess. A little."

"Well, Jerry's never sad. He's the happiest person on campus. Come on. Maybe if we get him to talk about his problems, they'll go away and he'll be happy again."

The woman took my hand and pulled me towards the man. On the way to the bench she grabbed another woman's hand with her free one and said, "Come on, Betsy. We have to cheer up Jerry."

The woman said, "Okay, Ramah."

So, that was the name of this strange woman. Ramah.

Ramah and Betsy sat on the bench on either side of Jerry. Jerry didn't even react to their arrival, and just stared at the ground in front of him blankly.

Ramah twirled one of the curls on Jerry's head around her finger. She said in a girly voice, "What's the matter, Jerry?"

Betsy blew into his ear. "Jerry, what's wrong?"

Jerry leaned forward and sighed. A single tear fell from the corner of his eye onto the grass at his feet. He leaned back, wiped his eye with his finger, and said, "For the past two years, I have been one of the most serious students at this college. I have hungrily devoured the works of all the great playwrights as I pursued a degree in the dramatic arts. But all of my hard work has been done with an eye to the future, to life after college. Every night I have dreamed of walking out of the garden gates of this institution into the real world. College is a great place to dream. But I didn't want to dream. I wanted to work! I wanted a job in theater. But then... But then..."

He buried his head in his hands again and sobbed.

Betsy gently said, "But then what?"

Jerry looked up at the sky, tears streaming down his cheeks. He said, "But then I learned that women are paid eighty-two cents on the dollar for doing the same amount of work as men."

Betsy and Ramah look at the man with sympathy. Ramah said, "It must have been very upsetting for you to learn that."

Betsy said, "I am so sorry."

The two girls stroked his cheeks with the backs of their hands as he gazed ahead with a look of utter despair. He said, "How can I get a job now, knowing that my female counterparts will be paid eighteen percent less than me? I would feel so guilty under these conditions that I wouldn't be able to function. All the work I have done preparing for the real world, all of those great playwrights whose masterpieces I have read, it has all been a waste."

Jerry broke down crying as the girls continued to console him by blowing into his ears and stroking his cheeks with their fingers.

When he didn't stop crying Ramah turned to me and said, "Hey, Ryan, perhaps there is something you could say that would cheer Jerry up."

I muttered, "I've never been much of a people person. I don't know what I can do, unless..."

Struck by a sudden notion, I punched Jerry in the face.

The two girls jumped back, shocked.

Ramah cried, "Oh my God."

Betsy screamed, "How could you do that!"

But Jerry looked up at me with a bleeding nose, smiling. Quietly, he whispered, "Thank you."

Chapter 8

Ramah was so impressed at my having cured Jerry that sh invited me up to her dorm room.

As we made our way through the dorms, she seemed ver excited for something, and danced around as if her anticipatio was so great she couldn't remain still. This excited me, as I w sure I was going to get laid and finally lose my virginity.

But when we entered the spacious double, Ramah ignore the man sitting on an old couch, staring blankly into space. Sh pulled a clear plastic zip lock bag full of freshly cut white flowe from one of her pockets, removed two flowers, handed me on and kept the other for herself.

She put hers in her mouth. I just looked at mine and sai "What is this?"

"It's the best Lotus you've ever tasted. It comes from BC."

I shrugged and ate the flower.

Just as I swallowed, the door opened and three guys typical frat clothing, but covered in dirt, entered. Rama screamed with delight, "Oh my God!!!"

She ran up and hugged all three, jumping allover them li a dog excited to see its master. "Where were you?" She cried, was just about to text."

One of them motioned to another and said, "Jay needed stop off and dirt so we all did."

Ramah said, "Have you tried fertilizer water? It's much mo nutritious."

The one called Jay said, "Nah. I don't go for that. Dirt pt hair on your chest."

Ramah said, "Look, I swore by dirt. But then I read how bad it is for the environment, so I switched to fertilizer water. Now I think everybody should."

The first one to speak said, "I don't know. I've tried fertilizer water. I always still feel hungry after. I need more substance. I need the feel of my roots in the ground."

Ramah said, "Well, yeah, that is a problem. But other than that it's fine."

The third frat boy, who hadn't spoken yet, pointed at the man sitting on the couch and asked, "Who's that?"

Ramah turned to the man, and as if noticing him for the first time, said, "You know, Jim, I don't know."

She put her hands on her hips and scolded the seated man saying, "Now look at this! If you sit like that long enough, you are going to get rooted to the couch."

She lifted the man a bit. Sure enough, there were white roots coming out of his back and bottom, going into the couch. The three frat boys rushed to her assistance and all four lifted the seated man so that his roots slid all the way out of the cushion.

Ramah handed the man a paper pouch and in a scolding tone said, "That couch has no nutritional value. Here, put this fertilizer packet into a tub and soak in it instead. You'll feel much better."

The man took the pouch, said, "Thank you. Sorry for getting rooted to your couch," and left the room as if in a daze.

I had watched the whole scene with detached interest. You see, the lotus flower I had eaten had made me feel funny. Good funny.

Ramah took her plastic bag from her pocket again, took out a bunch of white flowers, and passed them around to the dirt-covered frat boys, who started eating right away without a word.

Ramah said, "Tastes good, right? It comes from BC.

Jim said, "BC? Like, planet Canada?"

"Yeah, exactly. They grow it in greenhouses there. Huge greenhouses that span the tundra. They grow the best lotus flower on Canada in BC!"

We continued to eat lotus flowers as we talked and laughed until at some point we noticed that Jim had crawled off into a corner, and was crying.

Ramah said, "Jim, what's wrong? Why do you wind up crying every time you eat lotus flowers?"

Jim sobbed as he said, "It's just that I'm on full tuition because I'm rich, so my parents are paying $500,000 a year to send me to this school. You'd think I'd spend my time studying and bettering myself so I can get a good job. But instead, I'm eating lotus flowers, and my grades are suffering because of it."

Ramah said, "Well, Jim. It's all part of a complete education. I mean, not everything you learn is going to be in a classroom."

Jim cried out, "No! With what this college costs, everything I learn should come from a classroom!!! I could get street smarts for free on the street. I feel so guilty."

Ramah said "Hmmm... Guilty, you say? Say, Ryan, do you think you can do that thing you did to Jerry again? To make Jim not feel guilty anymore this time?"

Stoned from the flowers I had eaten, I said, "What, you mean punch him in the face?"

Ramah answered as if the words I had spoken were completely new to her. She said, "Yes. Punch... him... in... the... face..."

I said "Well, there's really no trick to it. Any of you could do it."

Ramah said, "Oh no, I'm a pacifist."

I looked at the other two frat boys. At once both said, "Oh no, we're pacifists."

I shrugged and said, "Well, okay."

I walked up to Jim and punched him in the face. He stopped crying right away, looked up at me gratefully with a bloody nose, and said, "Thank you! Now I can eat lotus flowers again without feeling bad about blowing off my schoolwork and wasting my parents' money."

Jim gave me a big bear hug as everyone looked at me in awe.

Chapter 9

Word quickly spread across campus about the amazing feat I could perform. Now, I stood behind a small booth in Ramah's dorm room while a line of people waiting to see me went out the room and stretched around the hall.

I punched the student in front of me in the face. Blood dripped from his nose. With a tear in his eye he said, "Thank you. Now I no longer feel guilty for masturbating," and departed.

I called, "Next."

The next student in line stepped forward and handed me a dollar bill. He had a sad, angry look to him as he said, "I feel so guilty about my homophobic and racist thoughts. It's my parental upbringing, though. I can't help it."

I punched him in the face.

With blood dripping from his nose he said, "Oh, thank you! Now I don't mind being a homophobe and a racist."

The student stepped aside and I called, "Next."

The next student stepped forward and handed me a dollar. He said, "I was driving drunk, and hit a young child playing in the street. I panicked and drove away from the scene, and was never caught. I feel so guilty."

I punched him in the face.

This went on for some time. I needed to use the restroom so I moved the fingers of a paper clock with the words "I will return at..." printed on top to fifteen minutes from now and made my way to the bathrooms at the end of the hall, which were coed. I was just thinking about how I hadn't seen Ramah in a few days

hen I entered the restroom which, oddly enough, had bathtubs
ing along the wall. They were all empty except for one, which

Ramah sat in, her white roots floating in the water and
nging over the tub.

She had a look of suffering on her face as she stared up at me
d said, "Oh, Ryan. I am so hungry."

Knowing a bit about how this world worked by this point I
id, "Well, why don't you go dirt?"

She climbed out of the tub and cried, "Don't tell me to dirt!
was men telling me to dirt that made me not want to dirt in
e first place."

She stood there naked, covered from neck to knee in white
ots that barely hid her body from my view. She was very thin,
aciated in fact.

Suddenly, a vulnerable look came upon her face and she
rst into tears. "I'm so hungry, though. Just look at me! I've lost
much body mass since I started using fertilizer water, as my
ots have grown longer and longer, searching for soil they will
ver find. I have wasted away to flesh and root, Ryan. Flesh and
ot! If this keeps up, soon I will be nothing but root."

She buried her head in her hands.

I put a hand on her shoulder and gently said, "Let me punch
u in the face."

She pulled away and cried, "No!"

"I won't even charge you a dollar. It'll be on me."

"But you don't understand! I grew up in a family where I was
nstantly told being pretty was the most important thing. And
ing pretty meant being thin. I can't dirt. I'd feel..."

She didn't finish her sentence, so I finished it for her.
uilty?" I said. "You'd feel guilty?"

Ramah gave me a needful look, sighed, and said, "Oka
Ryan. Punch me in the face."

I punched her. She looked up with tears of gratitude in h
eyes and blood dripping from her nose. "Thank you, Ryan. O.
thank you."

I left the restroom and was returning to work thinking abo
how ironic it was that I had finally found a job that I like
when men with black ski masks covering their faces, with b
machineguns, rushed down the hall and grabbed me. One p
a bag over my head, and I was dragged, kicking and screamin
from the dorms.

They took me outside and I was marched some ways. Whe
they took the bag off my head, I was in a small, well-decorate
office facing a muscular, middle-aged man with white hair. T
masked men departed.

The man said, "Greetings, Ryan, I am Dean Andrews."

There was a graph at his side, depicting a zigzagging line. H
pointed a pointer at the graph and said, "This line represen
guilt. As you can see, our college has experienced consecuti
rising levels of guilt every year until early this month, when f
the first time in our history, we saw a decline in guilt."

For most of the graph the line went on a steady upwa
trajectory, but then took a downward plunge at the very er
where he pointed, descending into flames.

The dean clenched his fists in anger. "These numbers a
unacceptable. Up until this semester our college has ranked to
ten in guilt in US News and Report. What is your secret? Ho
do you rid people of their guilt?"

I shouted, "Go to Hell!"

The dean picked up a scalpel from a white cloth on his desk and scraped it across the side of a coffee mug slowly from top to bottom. It made a horrible scraping noise that made me wince, and blood oozed down the ceramic where it was cut. The mug cried, "Ahahahaha!!!"

The dean brandished the scalpel at me and shouted, "I'm not joking around. I'll cut you too. Talk!"

I said, "Wait a minute. Why do you want the students to feel guilty?"

"I'll tell you why! Do you know what the purpose of college is?"

"Of course. It's, uh, well, you know, actually, that's a tough one. To educate, I guess?"

"No. The purpose of college is to get our students jobs, and the way we do that is guilt! We make you feel guilty, but refuse to punish you. Then when you graduate, you crave punishment, and take the first punishing job you find.

"But you, Ryan, have discovered some way to make the students not feel guilt. How can we mold our students into ideal citizens now? You have subverted our mission. I can't let you stay here. Not knowing how to do whatever it is you do."

The dean handed me a rolled-up piece of paper tied with a little bow. I looked at it, and then back up at the dean. "What's this?"

"This, Ryan, is a diploma. Congratulations. You have graduated college."

I cried, "Noooooo!!!"

Chapter 10

The masked men with the machineguns returned. They forced me into a black gown and placed a square black cap on my head. All the while I screamed, "Have a heart! It's not time yet. I still got time!"

The masked men dragged me to the door of the office as I pushed against the floor with my feet crying, "You can't do this to me. I have rights!"

The dean said, "Now, come on Ryan, don't make this any harder on yourself."

"But I'm not ready. I won't go without a fight," I said, as I thrashed around madly.

"You knew you'd have to get a job eventually," said the dean.

I stopped fighting and said, "Did you say... did you say job???"

I remembered then the office planet, and Destiny, and how I was living in dread over not knowing what had happened to her, hoping for the best but fearing the worst. The employees at that job, craving punishment, were exactly the kind of ideal citizen the dean claimed his college produced. Could the workforce on that planet have come from this one?

I stopped fighting, and allowed myself to be dragged out of the building to a field where hundreds of other students in black gowns and caps stood clutching their diplomas.

We were lead in a procession, as a marching band on either side of us played the Pomp and Circumstance March. We marched in a straight line for some time, until we entered the mouth of a large cave.

We continued to march through the cave, and although the band did not follow us inside, the Pomp and Circumstance March continued to play, as if the music arose out of thin air.

Within the cave was twilight, and little lights like will o' the wisps appeared at the feet of some of the graduates. The graduates followed their lights, which led them to small manholes carved into the floor of the cave. The graduates walked right up to the holes they were led to, stepped into them, and clutching their diplomas, disappeared into the earth.

A light appeared at my feet. I followed it to a hole, and following the example of the other graduates, stepped into it. My butt landed on a long and twisting chute, and I slid down, down, down into the bowels of the earth.

The chute dropped me in a cushioned, straight-backed chair, still clutching my diploma. Bent out of shape from the rapid turns of the slide, I took a moment to recover my senses.

I looked around, and saw that I was in the reception area of an office suite. All along the walls were chairs just like the one I sat in, and sitting in the chairs were young recent college graduates just like myself, clutching their diplomas nervously as they waited. I wondered what we were waiting for. There were shaft openings in the ceiling above each office chair, and sometimes a recent college graduate would fall from one, clutching his diploma, and land seated in a chair.

A beautiful woman in a sharp business suit entered the reception area through ornately carved oak doors that led into the office suite. She looked at a clipboard and then called a name. A tall, skinny man leapt to his feet, gulped, and said, "That's me."

The woman said, "Come this way."

With sweat pouring down his brow, the young man nervously followed her through the oak doors.

I let out a cry of despair. This was a planet of wage slaves, but it wasn't my planet of wage slaves. The decor was all wrong. My office planet was low-rent. This one was upscale. In my office planet, the seats made your back ache and you expected to get bedbugs from sitting on them. The upholstery on the seats here was attractive, comfortable, and vermin-free. In my office planet, the white paint was peeling off the walls. The walls of this one had a fresh coat of cream-colored paint. Here, framed reproductions of classical paintings hung from the walls. On my planet, the walls were covered with ripped and torn motivational posters, many of which contained misspellings.

Finally, Ryan's name was called. Having nothing else to do, I rose and followed the smartly-dressed woman past rows and rows of small offices where job interviews were taking place, until she stopped at one and motioned for me to enter. I did, and seated behind the desk was Destiny. My heart skipped a beat. I muttered, "How... how is it possible?"

She glanced up, and then without seeming to recognize me asked, "Is this your first job interview?"

Answering honestly, I said, "Yes."

"Well, have a seat."

I sat down, dejected. Had I meant so little to Destiny that she had already forgotten about me?

She held out her hand and said, "Diploma?"

I gave her the scroll. She unrolled it, looked it over, and said, "Hmmm. That's a good school. I see you just recently graduated. Do you have a resume?"

"No."

"Well, that's okay. So..." She looked back down at the diploma and read the name there, "Ryan. I am going to give you script to read out loud. This is just to test your reading skills, so there is no need to 'act.' Just read in a neutral voice."

Then I realized why she didn't recognize me. I wasn't in my own body, or the body of Roger. I was in the body of a recent college grad named Ryan.

I whispered, "Psst. Destiny. It's me, Richard."

Her jaw dropped momentarily. She said, "Ri... Ri... Richard???"

I told her how on planet Los Angeles there was another portal that brought me to the college planet, and how I graduated and wound up here.

She said, "Yes. I was playing around with my bio signature reader and I discovered someone that had just arrived at college who had the same bio signature as you. So, I sent a portal through another portal to planet Los Angeles honed in on your bio signature, hoping you would find it and jump into it. The reason I was caught off guard just now is I didn't know Ryan's name, what he looked like, or when he was graduating."

I said, "Okay. That explains where the second portal came from, but there is so much that hasn't been explained. Like, how did you have access to a portal that took you to planet Los Angeles, and how did you have a car when you got there, and how did you get a bio reader?"

Destiny said, "All those questions can be answered by reading this."

She slid a book across the desk. It was a huge book, as big as a phone book. I looked at the title. It was, "How to organize an insurrection."

I opened the book to chapter one and read:

> Welcome to the wild and wonderful world of insurrections. Human beings have organizing insurrections for thousands of years to help accomplish all sorts of important goals. The first insurrections were organized over three thousand years ago in ancient China during the Ming Dynasty. The Chinese used insurrections to overthrow many important institutions, from farming, to trade, to palace administration.
>
> In this book, you will learn everything you need to know to be empowered to organize an insurrection of your own.

I slammed the book shut, looked up, and said, "I am not readi this shit! Just tell me how I got from the college planet to th one."

"They are both the same planet. The liberal arts college on the surface, while the corporation is beneath the earth. T corporation uses the college to supply its labor force."

"Oh, that's really smart of them," I said. "That way they c recruit all the best students, and leave the rest for oth corporations."

"Oh no," said Destiny. "They don't want the A students. They're the smartest, and ask too many questions the corporation doesn't want to answer."

"Oh," I said, wrinkling my brow in concentration as I thought this over. "So... they hire the worst students, then?"

"No. They don't want them either. The D and F students are loyal, but they aren't competent enough to do the actual work."

I thought some more, puzzled. "Oh!" I said as the light bulb finally went off in my head. "They hire the ones in the middle!!!"

"That's right! The C students are smart enough to do the job, but not so smart that they'll get bored and challenge the status quo."

I said, "But how did you wind up here? What happened after I...?"

Destiny said, "After Goodwyn's supervisors shot you, your life force returned to your own body on planet Los Angeles, and was replaced by Roger's. With his last dying breath Roger said, 'I... I stole your lunch.' The supervisors checked his corpse and sure enough, in one of his jacket pockets was a tuna fish sandwich in a brown paper bag with 'Goodwyn' written on the outside in black sharpie. Goodwyn's lunch must have been on your person the whole time, but you didn't know it because Roger had stolen it before you took over his body."

"Wow," I said. "That's an amazing story. But how did you get here, to this office planet?"

"It's all the same planet."

"But everything is so upscale!"

"That's just because you are in a reception area. The places that visitors see look nice to keep up appearances. The inner offices where only employees go are kept a dump, to break our spirits."

I said, "Then bring me to Goodwyn, so I can defeat him."

She looked away tearfully and said, "No. I can't. Not after what happened last time. That dream is over. The reason I brought you this time was not to overthrow Goodwyn. It was because I want to be with you, forever. I couldn't bear to lose you again."

"I have learned a lot since my last encounter with Goodwyn," I said. "I know what to do now."

I guess she saw the determination in my voice or face because she nodded and said, "Okay, *Ryan*." She said the name Ryan with a wink. "You're hired."

She handed me an index card with the word "Trainee" written on it, in a plastic sleeve with a clip on the back. She said, "Here, take this badge and clip it to your collar. As long as you wear it over your breast, you shall have free passage. Let's go."

Destiny led me down some halls. As we went, I recognized the griminess of the office planet I knew. We opened an office door where we heard moaning, to see if Goodwyn was there. There was no Goodwyn, but five nude women chained standing to racks. Their arms and legs were stretched painfully by the devices as they moaned in pain.

I wanted to rescue them but Destiny said, "No. We cannot lose sight of the bigger picture. Once we defeat Goodwyn, all will be free."

We went on some more down the depressing halls, until we heard the voice of Goodwyn coming from inside an office as he shouted, "I am sick and tired of being disgusted every time I go to the bathroom, and I am going to beat her again and again until one of you tells me!"

I opened the door. There was Goodwyn with a riding whip, standing in front of a completely nude woman. Her hands were secured above her head to a chain that hung from the ceiling, and her feet were lifted so that she had to stretch to make her big toes touch the ground and give her body some support. Her body was covered in fresh welts and bruises. Goodwyn brought the riding whip back as he shouted, "Who has been putting paper towels in the waterless urinal?"

I walked up to Goodwyn before he could strike the woman and punched him in the face. He stumbled back as the supervisors pointed their machineguns at me.

Goodwyn said, "Don't shoot him."

The supervisors held their fire.

Goodwyn looked up at me. With blood dripping from his nose he whispered, "Thank you."

Goodwyn then turned to the office and said, "I, Lawrence J. Goodwyn, having been cured of my guilty feelings which compelled me to subjugate all of you, hereby proclaim your manumission, effective immediately!"

The entire office gave out a roaring cheer in reply.

Destiny put her arms around my neck, gave me a big kiss, and said, "You did it! You really did it! I always knew you would."

"And ironically," I said, "It was college that finally prepared me for the real world."

Also by J. Manfred Weichsel

Watch for more at
https://j-manfred-weichsel.mailchimpsites.com/.

About the Author

J. Manfred Weichsel writes satires that fuse adventure, horror, science fiction, and fantasy into some of the most original transgressive literature being published today.

Weichsel began writing short fiction in 2016 with stories that have appeared in some of the biggest titles of the new pulp movement, such as Cirsova Magazine and the Planetary Anthology series.

When the pandemic hit, Weichsel was suddenly jobless but—thanks to government handouts—making more than he had been when working. He decided to treat his situation as an opportunity and began writing longer works and learning how to self-publish.

Now a fiercely independent author, J. Manfred Weichsel aims to fulfill the promise of self-publishing with works ungoverned by the constraints of traditional publishing houses and the inhibitions of polite society.

Loved by some and hated by others, Weichsel's funny, unconventional, often grotesque books inhabit a unique space in American literature and will be read, talked about, and debated for generations to come.

Read more at https://j-manfred-weichsel.mailchimpsites.com/.

Lightning Source UK Ltd.
Milton Keynes UK
UKHW010440090223
416681UK00003B/885

9 798215 161173